my name is SANGOEL

Written by
Karen Lynn Williams **and** Khadra Mohammed

Illustrated by
Catherine Stock

Eerdmans Books for Young Readers

Grand Rapids, Michigan • Cambridge, U.K.

For Jennifer W., whose editorial comments helped make this book come
true. And in memory of my grandfather, whose last name was changed
when he immigrated to the United States.
— *K.L.W.*

For Younos, Mohamed, and Ibrahim, my sons, and to all
refugee boys in search of a place to call home.
— *K.M.*

For my godson William, who also has African roots.
— *C.S.*

Text © 2009 Karen Lynn Williams and Khadra Mohammed
Illustrations © 2009 Catherine Stock

Published in 2009 by Eerdmans Books for Young Readers
an imprint of Wm. B. Eerdmans Publishing Co.

Wm. B. Eerdmans Publishing Co.
2140 Oak Industrial Dr. NE, Grand Rapids, Michigan 49505
P.O. Box 163, Cambridge CB3 9PU U.K.

www.eerdmans.com/youngreaders

Manufactured in Singapore

14 13 12 11 10 09   9 8 7 6 5 4 3 2 1

Library of Congress Cataloging-in-Publication Data

Williams, Karen Lynn.
My name is Sangoel / by Karen Lynn Williams and Khadra Mohammed ; illustrated by Catherine Stock.
p. cm.
Summary: As a refugee from Sudan to the United States, Sangoel is frustrated that no one can
pronounce his name correctly until he finds a clever way to solve the problem.
ISBN 978-0-8028-5307-3 (alk. paper)
[1. Communication — Fiction. 2. Names, Personal — Fiction. 3. Immigrants — Fiction.
4. Refugees — Fiction. 5. Sudanese Americans — Fiction.]
I. Williams, Karen Lynn. II. Stock, Catherine, ill. III. Title.
PZ7.M727455My 2009
[E] —dc22
                    2008031735

"Don't worry," the Wise One said as Sangoel prepared to leave the refugee camp. "You carry a Dinka name. It is the name of your father and of your ancestors before him."

The old man hugged him, and Sangoel could feel the bones in his thin arms. "Remember, you will always be a Dinka. You will be Sangoel. Even in America."

Sangoel's father was killed in the war in Sudan. His family had to run from the fighting in the middle of the night. Sangoel was a refugee. He did not have a home. He did not have a country.

Many people in the camp were waiting to be resettled, but the Wise One could not leave. No country wanted one who was too old to work.

"In America you will have a new home," Sangoel's friends told him. "You will never again have to escape in the night."

Everyone waved good-bye. Sangoel's little sister, Lili, cried. Silent tears rolled down Mama's cheeks. Sangoel knew he would never see his friends again.

The "sky boat" took them to America.

Everywhere, people rushed around, speaking English very fast.
The stairs in the airport moved, and Mama was afraid to step
on them. Doors opened by magic. Bright flashing lights made
Sangoel's eyes burn. He shivered and his head ached.

"There, Mama, look!" he shouted. "Our name!" He spoke in Dinka, the language of his ancestors, and pointed across the huge room.

Sangoel was only eight, but he was the man of the family. He grabbed Mama's hand and pulled her and Lili through the crowd. He stopped in front of the woman who held the sign.

She smiled at Sangoel. "You must be . . ." She frowned and looked at a paper in her hand . . . "San-go-el."

Sangoel shook his head and kept his eyes on the floor. "My name is Sangoel," he said softly in the simple English he had learned in the camp.

"I am Mrs. Johnson," the woman said. "Welcome to America." She threw her arms around Mama and Lili. She bent down and squeezed Sangoel. She smelled like flowers. Mama and Mrs. Johnson were both crying. Sangoel blinked back tears.

America was big and open and free. There was no barbed wire to keep them in.

Mrs. Johnson showed them how to cross the street. All the cars stopped when the light was red, but Mama would not move until Mrs. Johnson helped her.

Their new home was called an apartment. Mrs. Johnson brought a big bag of used clothes. She showed Mama how to cook on the stove. Sangoel translated. Everyone practiced pushing the buttons on the telephone. They learned how to eat with forks.

The TV was a box with real people inside. Lili cried when Sangoel turned it on. She cried again when he turned it off.

The next day Mrs. Johnson took Sangoel for a check-up.
The doctor stared at the medical form and scrunched up her
forehead. "Sang-o-el. How are you?"

"My name is Sangoel," he mumbled. "I am well." The
doctor nodded and listened to his heart. Her hands were cold.

When it was time to go to school, Sangoel did not want to
leave Mama and Lili. But Mama said, "You must go to school."
Sangoel remembered the words of the Wise One:
"Education is your mother and your father."

The teacher gave him his own desk. But when she
introduced him to the class, she scrunched up her forehead,
trying to read his name. "This is San, Sang, San-go-el."

"San-Sang," the girl next to him called out. The kids
laughed. Sangoel lowered his head. He remembered the
Wise One's words and held his anger inside.

"My name is Sangoel," he whispered, but no one heard.

Mrs. Johnson signed him up for football, but in America they called it soccer. Everyone on the team got a brand-new shirt, as blue as the sky in Sudan.

Sangoel lined up with the other boys, and the coach called out each of their names. When he frowned at the paper, Sangoel knew whose name he would call next.

"My name is Sangoel," he said before the coach could say it wrong.

As Sangoel walked home from practice, one of his
teammates ran up. "Hey, Sango."

"My name is Sangoel," he called softly as the boy ran off.

Sangoel wore his new soccer shirt that night at dinner, but he still wasn't happy. The rice stuck in his throat and he wished he were back at the camp.

"What's the matter?" Mama asked.

"In America I have lost my name."

Mama sighed. Her eyes were sad. "America is our home now. Perhaps you need an American name."

The words of the Wise One sang in his memory. *You will always be Sangoel.*

That night Sangoel slept on a rug on the floor instead of in his American bed. He had bad dreams about war and running and hiding.

In the morning Lili giggled and pointed to the letters on his shirt.

"Dynamo," Sangoel told her. He straightened his shoulders.

"It is my team name. See the ball?"

Then Sangoel had an idea. He dumped all of the clothes out of the bag Mrs. Johnson had brought. In the pile he found an almost-white shirt. He got his school markers and went to work.

Finally, Sangoel put the markers away. He took off his brand-new soccer shirt. He put on his almost-white shirt and went to school.

All the children crowded around to read Sangoel's shirt. "My name is," it said across the top. After the words there were two pictures.

"It's a sun and a soccer ball," the boy named Billy said.

"It's a goal," the girl next to him said. "Your name is Sun-goal."

Sangoel nodded and smiled.

The girl took a piece of paper out of her desk. She made a quick design and held it up.

"I am . . ."

"Carmen," Sangoel said.

"Yessss!" The girl held two thumbs up.

Other students began tearing pages out of their notebooks and grabbing markers from their desks.

Across the room a boy held up his paper. "My name is Jason."

"I'm Keesha." Another girl waved her picture like a flag.

Toby drew a toe and a bee.

"You had a good idea, Sangoel." His teacher gave him a big smile. "And you have a very good name."

He stood tall and proud. "It is the name of my father and my grandfather and his father before him," he said. "My name is Sangoel. Even in America."

Authors' Note

People who are forced to leave their homes and seek protection in a new country are called refugees. There are more than 30 million refugees in the world today. Most of them are women and children.

Refugees like Sangoel flee their country because of war or persecution based on race, religion, or political ideas. A refugee often has to leave home at a moment's notice and may not be able to bring along family members, money, clothing, or food.

A refugee camp is a large guarded area where people are forced to stay until they find a country that will give them a home. Families live in tents or huts and have little to eat. Often there are no schools, no electricity, and no clean drinking water.

Refugees come from many countries. Sangoel is from the Dinka tribe in southern Sudan, which is the largest country in Africa. Years of war and persecution have forced many people to leave Sudan.

In some cultures like the Dinka, the firstborn son carries the name of his ancestors as his first name. That name is also his last name, and he might have a middle name as well. So Sangoel could have the name Sangoel Jukib Sangoel, for example.

For many years people coming to the United States to make a new home were given Americanized names. Today more people choose to keep the name that connects them to their heritage.